MEASURING A YEAR

A Rosh Hashanah Story

by **Linda Elovitz Marshall**

illustrations by **Zara González Hoang**

Abrams Appleseed • New York

How do you measure a year?
By looking at how much you grew . . .

. . . or all the things you learned to do?

Through pictures,
stories,
things you made,

SLIME!

kids you met,

or places stayed?

Trees you planted,
flowers grown,

a move away,
a brand-new home?

Times you were sad

Times you were strong

and super brave?

Things you wish
you hadn't said

or that you
hadn't done?

Times when everything was right

and everyone had fun?

Weddings?
Bar mitzvahs?
Times making
new friends . . .

. . . or coming home when
travel ends?

Our lives have changed
in many ways.

So on these special holidays,
we give thanks for being here
and wish each other
a sweet New Year!

Shana Tova!

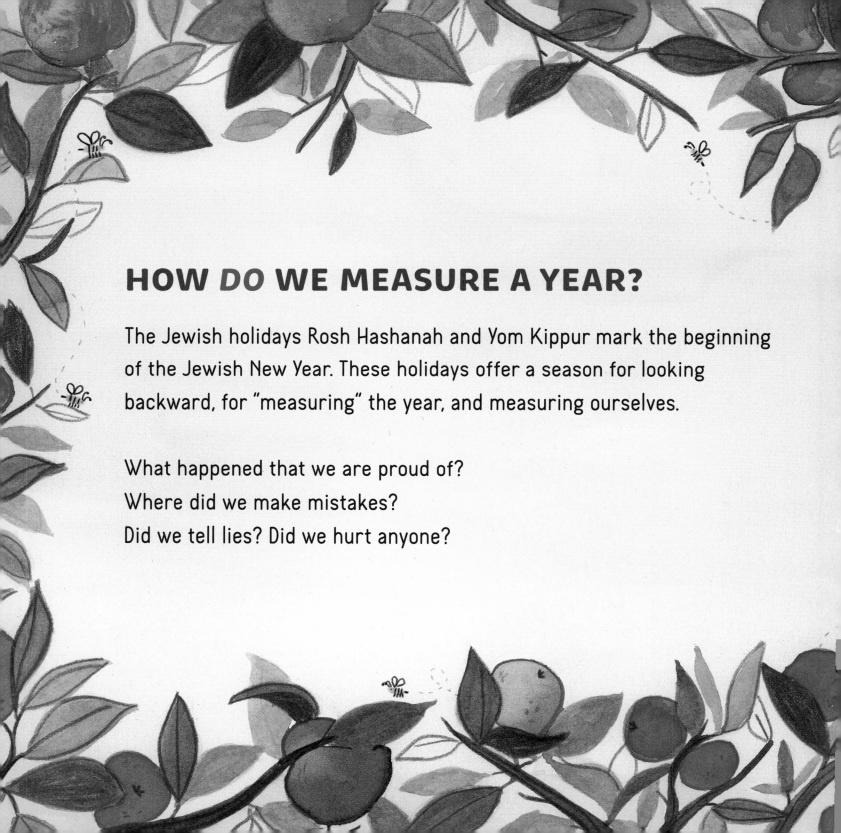

HOW *DO* WE MEASURE A YEAR?

The Jewish holidays Rosh Hashanah and Yom Kippur mark the beginning of the Jewish New Year. These holidays offer a season for looking backward, for "measuring" the year, and measuring ourselves.

What happened that we are proud of?
Where did we make mistakes?
Did we tell lies? Did we hurt anyone?

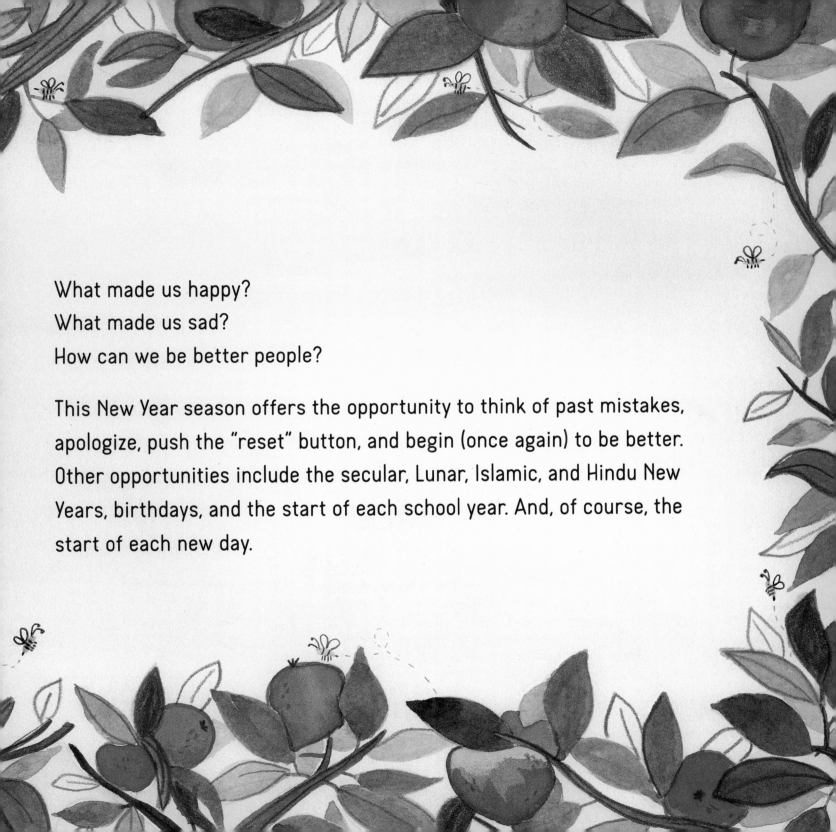

What made us happy?
What made us sad?
How can we be better people?

This New Year season offers the opportunity to think of past mistakes, apologize, push the "reset" button, and begin (once again) to be better. Other opportunities include the secular, Lunar, Islamic, and Hindu New Years, birthdays, and the start of each school year. And, of course, the start of each new day.

To my children and grandchildren for their help measuring years
in such delightful ways: Dena, Jonah, Benjamin, Rebecca, Gabriel, Niomi,
Julia Rose, Avigail, Lyra, Talia, Leah, Noa, Baruch, Ezra, Aviya, Orly,
Ellie, David, Sarai, and those yet to come.

And most especially to the late Cantor Jodi Schechtman of Congregation
Beth Emeth in Albany, New York, for her inspiration and encouragement.
—L.E.M.

To my mom, for passing down the traditions that help me measure the years.
—Z.G.H.

The artwork for this book was created using watercolor, colored pencils, and a bit of Photoshop magic.

Cataloging-in-Publication Data has been applied for and may be obtained from the Library of Congress.

ISBN 978-1-4197-4497-6

Text © 2022 Linda Elovitz Marshall
Illustrations © 2022 Zara González Hoang
Book design by Heather Kelly

Printed and bound in China
10 9 8 7 6 5 4 3 2

For bulk discount inquiries, contact specialsales@abramsbooks.com.

ABRAMS The Art of Books
195 Broadway, New York, NY 10007
abramsbooks.com